Fiona French won the 1986 Kate Greenaway Medal for her book
Snow White in New York. In 1992, *Anancy and Mr Dry-Bone,* her first
book for Frances Lincoln, was selected for Children's Book of the Year
and won the Sheffield Book Award. *Pepi and the Secret Name*s,
written by Jill Paton Walsh, was described by *Child Education* as
"stunning, a superb example of Fiona French at her very best,"
and chosen as one of their Best Story Books of 1994. *Little Inchkin,*
Lord of the Animals, Jamil's Clever Cat and Joyce Dunbar's
The Glass Garden, published during the 1990s, all reflect
Fiona's wide-ranging illustrative styles. Her latest books are
a series of illuminated texts from the King James Bible:
Bethlehem, Easter and *Paradise*.

To Harry and Jenny

Anancy and Mr Dry-Bone copyright © Frances Lincoln Limited 1991
Text and illustrations copyright © Fiona French 1991

First published in Great Britain in 1991 by Frances Lincoln Children's Books,
4 Torriano Mews, Torriano Avenue, London NW5 2RZ
www.franceslincoln.com

This paperback edition published in Great Britain and the USA in 2007

British Library Cataloguing in Publication Data available on request

ISBN 978-1-84507-164-6

Illustrated with mixed media

Printed in China

9 8 7 6 5 4 3 2 1

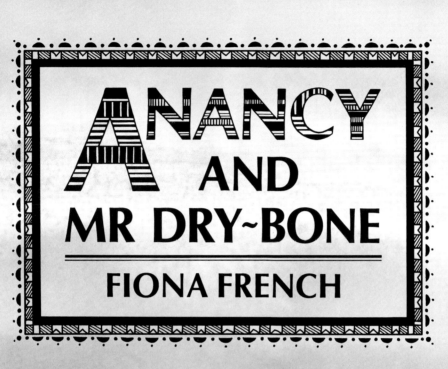

ANANCY
AND
MR DRY~BONE

FIONA FRENCH

F

FRANCES LINCOLN
CHILDREN'S BOOKS

Mr Dry-Bone lived in a big house
on top of a hill.
He was very rich and he wanted
to marry Miss Louise.

Anancy lived in a small house
at the foot of the hill.
He was very poor and he wanted to
marry Miss Louise as well.

Miss Louise lived on the other side of the hill.
She wasn't rich and she wasn't poor.
She was very <u>clever</u> and very very beautiful.
But Miss Louise had never laughed
in her whole life, so the first man
who could make her laugh,
that was the one she'd marry.

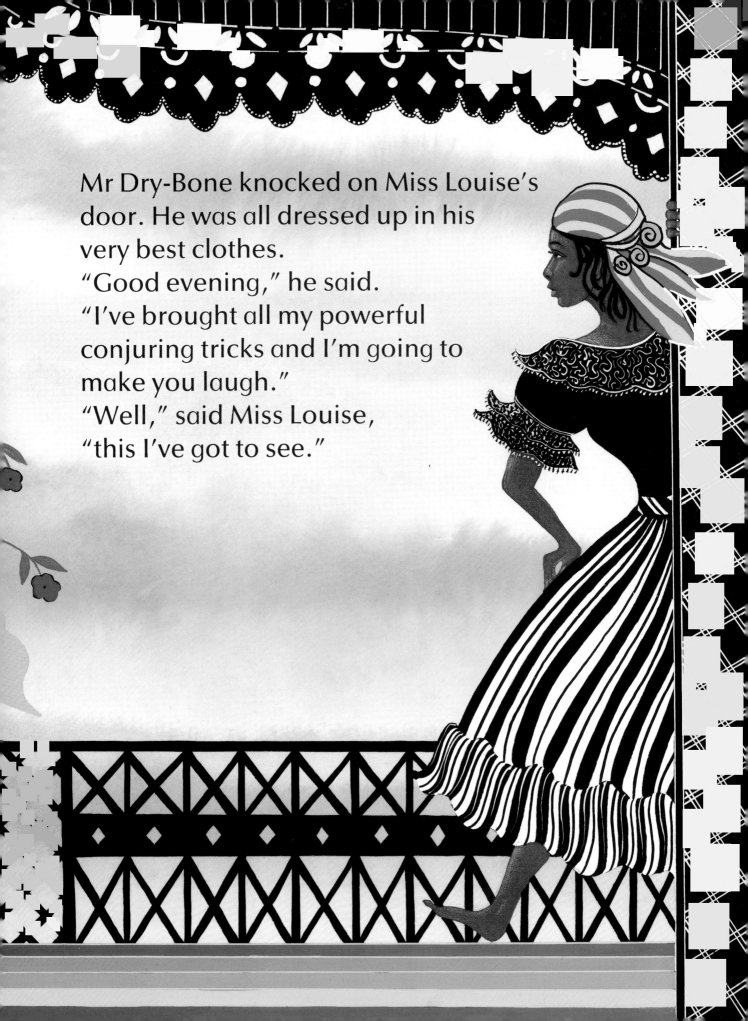

Mr Dry-Bone knocked on Miss Louise's
door. He was all dressed up in his
very best clothes.
"Good evening," he said.
"I've brought all my powerful
conjuring tricks and I'm going to
make you laugh."
"Well," said Miss Louise,
"this I've got to see."

Mr Dry-Bone turned himself into a bat
that flapped and a cat that spat;
he turned himself into a pig that honked
and a rabbit that did nothing.
But Miss Louise never smiled.

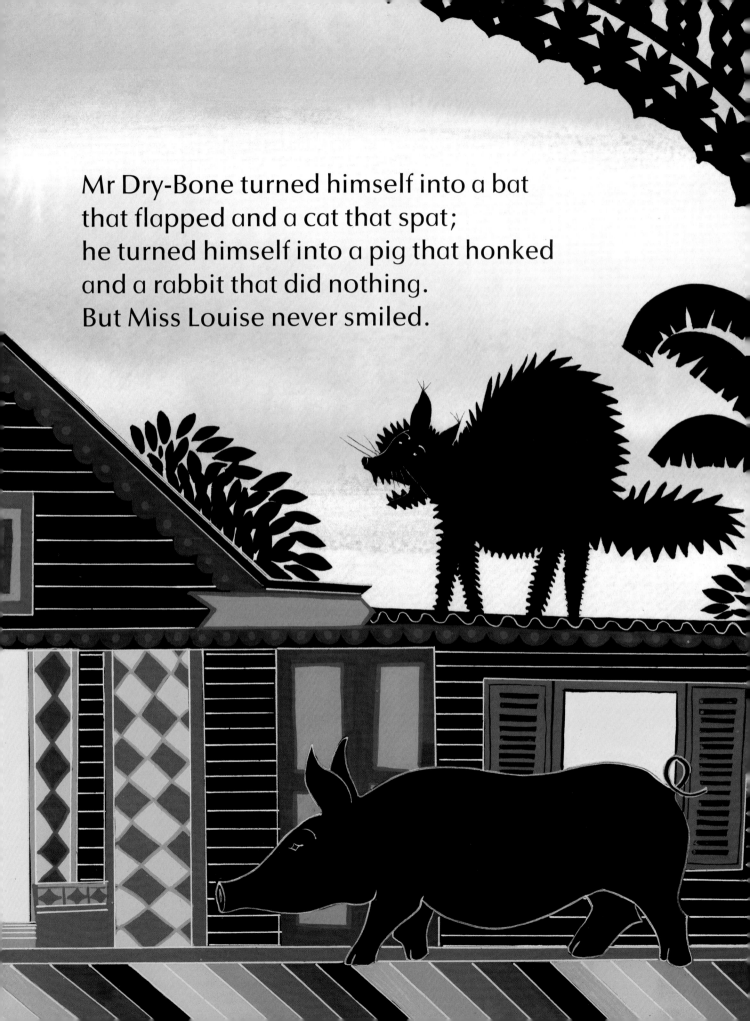

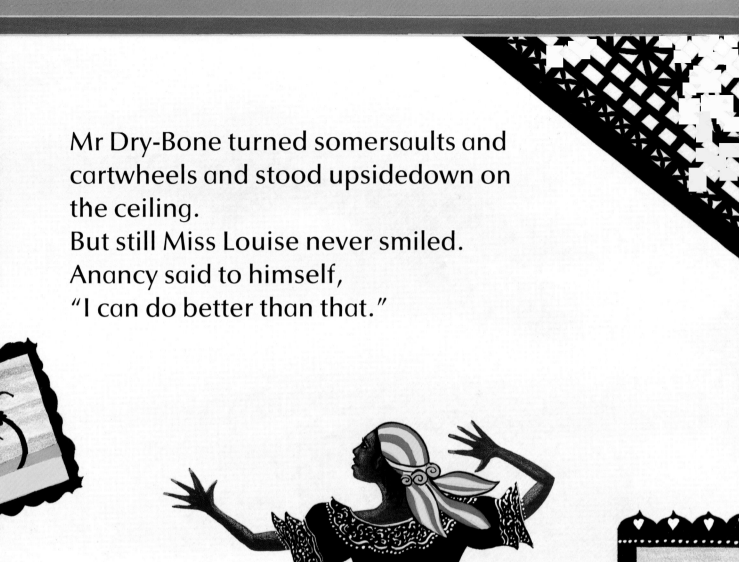

Mr Dry-Bone turned somersaults and
cartwheels and stood upsidedown on
the ceiling.
But still Miss Louise never smiled.
Anancy said to himself,
"I can do better than that."

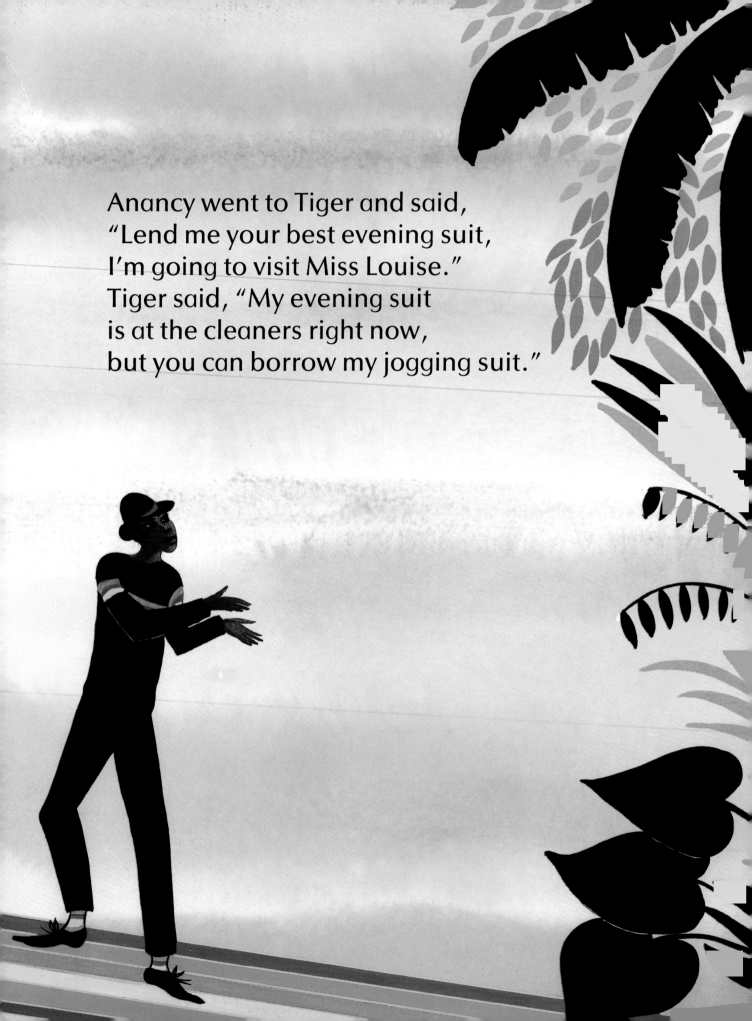

Anancy went to Tiger and said,
"Lend me your best evening suit,
I'm going to visit Miss Louise."
Tiger said, "My evening suit
is at the cleaners right now,
but you can borrow my jogging suit."

Anancy went to see Dog.
"Lend me your top hat,
I'm going to visit Miss Louise."
Dog said, "My top hat got
crushed the other day but
you can borrow my
hunting hat."

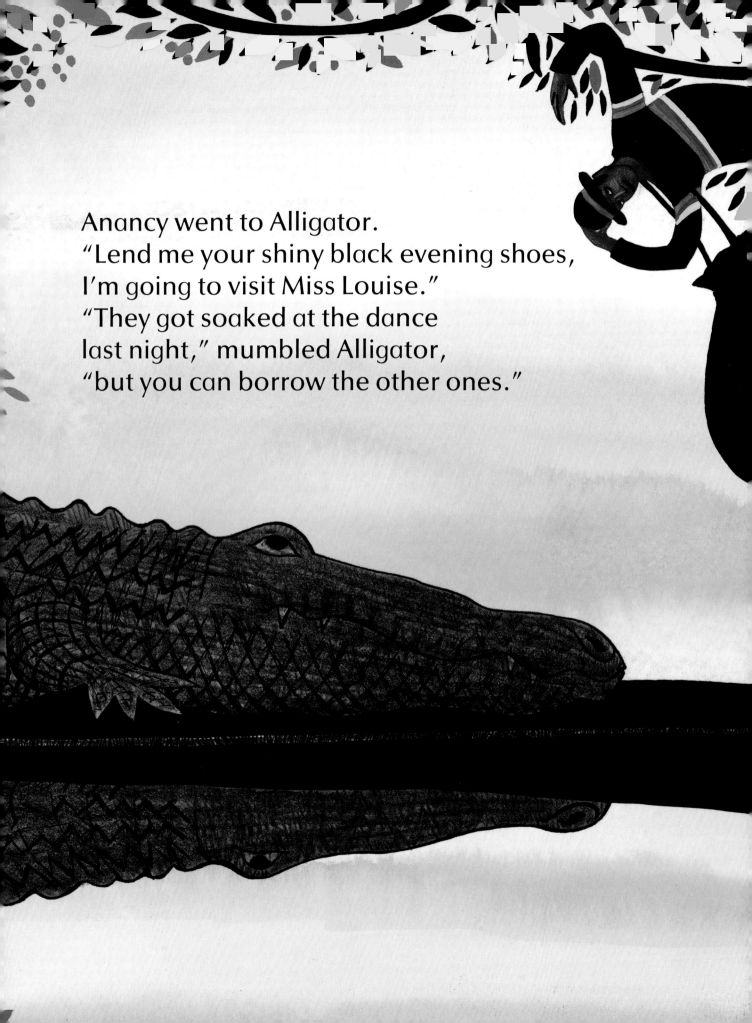

Anancy went to Alligator.
"Lend me your shiny black evening shoes,
I'm going to visit Miss Louise."
"They got soaked at the dance
last night," mumbled Alligator,
"but you can borrow the other ones."

Monkey swung through the trees
and called to Anancy,
"You'll need a tie when you
visit Miss Louise."

Parrot squawked and dropped
some feathers.
"Put these in your hunting hat, Anancy,
they'll look real good when you
visit Miss Louise."

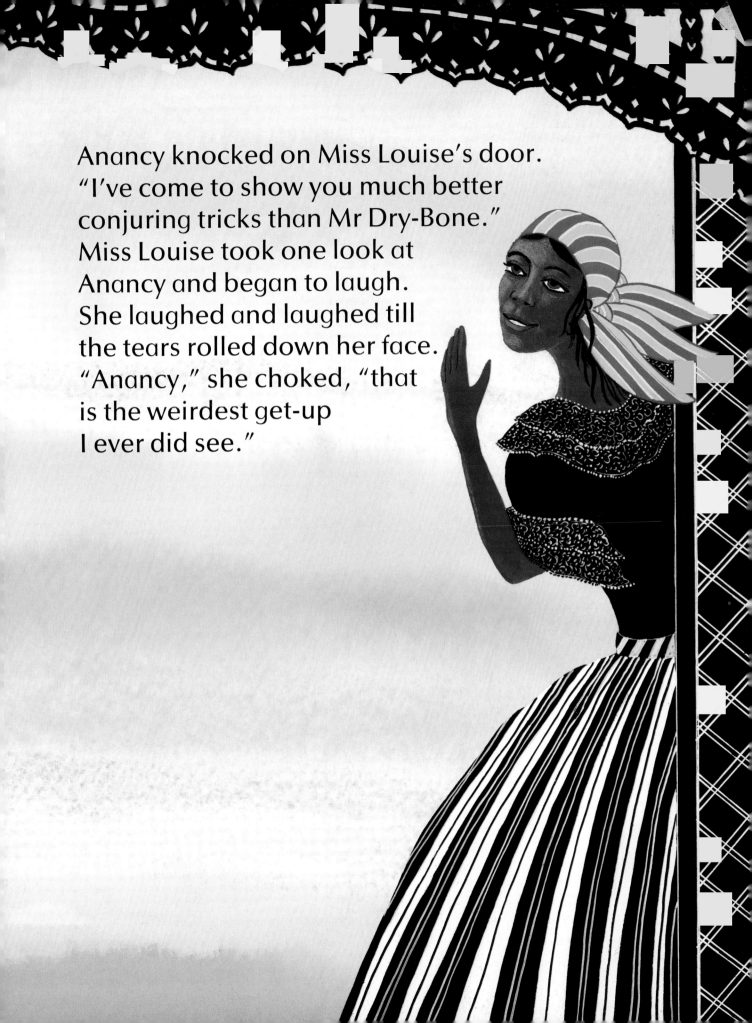

Anancy knocked on Miss Louise's door. "I've come to show you much better conjuring tricks than Mr Dry-Bone." Miss Louise took one look at Anancy and began to laugh. She laughed and laughed till the tears rolled down her face. "Anancy," she choked, "that is the weirdest get-up I ever did see."

Everyone laughed.
Even Mr Dry-Bone.
"OK, you win," he said.

So Anancy married Miss Louise,
and they all lived happily
ever after.

MORE TITLES FROM
FRANCES LINCOLN CHILDREN'S BOOKS

Jamil's Clever Cat
Fiona French with Dick Newby

Sardul is the cleverest of cats. When he learns that his master,
Jamil the weaver, dreams of marrying a princess, he resolves to make
Jamil's wish come true. But how can he make Jamil appear
the richest man in the world, and so win the princess's hand?

ISBN 978-1-84507-518-7

Pepi and the Secret Names
Jill Paton Walsh
Illustrated by Fiona French

Prince Dhutmose has commanded a splendid tomb to be built
for his final journey to the Land of the Dead. Pepi's father is to
decorate it, but how can he paint the unimaginable – the
Lions of the Horizon, the terrible hawk-god Horus, and Mertseger
the deadly winged cobra? Pepi decides to find real-life models
for his father, using his knowledge of secret names…

ISBN 978-0-7112-1089-9 (UK)
ISBN 978-1-84507-315-2 (US)

Little Inchkin
Fiona French

Little Inchkin is only as big as a lotus flower, but he has the courage
of a Samurai warrior. How he proves his valour, wins the hand
of a princess, and is granted his dearest wish by the Lord Buddha
is charmingly retold in this Tom Thumb legend of Old Japan.

ISBN 978-0-7112-0917-6 (UK)
ISBN 978-1-84507-206-3 (US)

Frances Lincoln titles are available from all good bookshops.
You can also buy books and find out more about your favourite titles,
authors and illustrators on our website: www.franceslincoln.com